To Find a Dinosaur

Dorothy E. Shuttlesworth

To Find a Dinosaur

Doubleday & Company, Inc., Garden City, New York

ISBN: 0-385-02233-6 Trade
     0-385-04466-6 Prebound
Library of Congress Catalog Card Number 73–78093

For our Jennifer Lynn,
who is already beginning to
wonder about dinosaurs

ACKNOWLEDGMENTS

The author's deep appreciation goes to: Robert Salkin for sharing his experiences as a teacher of paleontology in elementary schools and for his critical reading of the manuscript; to Dr. Edwin H. Colbert for reading Chapter 10; to Louis Paul Jonas, Jr., for his assistance in telling the story of the World's Fair dinosaurs; to James M. Staples for his photographic safaris to obtain illustrations.

Contents

To Find a Dinosaur

1. The Mystery Bones

Dinosaurs seem to have returned to haunt the earth. Pictures of them are seen everywhere—in books, newspapers, magazines, and films. Visitors to large museums often find not only the fossil skeletons, but paintings, or murals, portraying the strange reptiles. And boys and girls, as soon as they begin the study of rocks and fossils, learn about dinosaurs.

What weird and wonderful animals they were! Mighty, towering Tyrannosaurus. Huge, bulky Brontosaurus. Small, fast-moving Coelophysis. And countless other kinds—from giants to midgets. It is not surprising that people are fascinated; those with an adventurous spirit would give almost anything to find a real, live dinosaur somewhere in the world.

Of course that is impossible. The last of the dinosaurs died more than sixty million years ago.

This fact alone makes the dinosaurs' story remarkable: They vanished long before there were people to make pictures of them or to write about them. Yet today it is possible to know what they looked like and how they behaved. How did this come about? And why was their existence in prehistoric times not suspected until quite recently?

The answers to these questions involve clues, as in a mystery story. Scientists were the detectives; fossils were their clues.

A serious study of fossil bones began early in the nineteenth century when a French scientist, Baron Georges Cuvier, turned his interest toward understanding the fossil remains of animals with backbones. For more than forty years he wrote about and published all the facts that became clear to him, and these publications served as a foundation for the science of vertebrate (backbone) paleontology (the study of ancient living things).

In England at about the same time, two learned men, Dr. Gideon Mantell and Sir Richard Owen, also were discovering and studying fossil bones. One day Dr. Mantell's wife was looking at rocks which had been badly cracked by weathering when she noticed some strange, big teeth. She carried them home to her husband, who was puzzled enough to send them to other scientists for their opinions. However, he was not satisfied with their conclusions. ("Rhinoceros teeth," they said.) He then took chisel and hammer and carefully went to work on the rocks where his wife had made her discovery.

There Dr. Mantell found a number of other fossil bones

Brontosaurus—one of the largest and most defenseless of all dinosaurs. *Courtesy, The American Museum of Natural History. Painting by Charles R. Knight.*

that surely belonged with the teeth. And further study convinced him that the "remains" were those of an extinct giant lizard. Since the teeth resembled those of a living lizard, the iguana, he named the ancient one "iguanodon."

Later, Richard Owen felt a more general name was needed to fit such extinct reptiles which were beginning to be revealed in the earth. Working with the skeletons of living animals, he gained a wide knowledge about all kinds of reptiles, and gradually he realized there were certain bones from a far distant era which should be classified as a separate group.

At a meeting of the British Association for the Advancement of Science, in 1841, Sir Richard suggested the name *Dinosauria*. Members of the Association agreed with his reasoning: In Greek *deinos* means "terrible"; *sauros* is "lizard."

From then on "dinosaurs" (simplified from *Dinosauria*) were recognized as a special kind of reptile. One distinction of their anatomy was having two openings on each side of the skull behind the eye. Other reptiles did not have this feature.

However, there was still much to be learned. Not all were big enough to be considered "terrible." Some were quite small. Many ate only vegetation—never flesh. And an important difference in anatomy divided dinosaurs into two main groups. In one, the hips were constructed in the pattern of reptiles' hips. In the other, the hip arrangement was similar to that of birds' hips.

It took time for these facts, and others, to be understood. Many more fossils had to be discovered, examined and discussed before a true picture of the life and times of the dinosaurs was reached. In the years that followed the creation of the name *Dinosauria,* numerous discoveries were made—in the United States, Canada, South America, Europe, Africa, Asia, and Australia.

The first American dinosaur to be "brought back to life" through fossils is called Hadrosaurus ("bulky lizard"). An accidental discovery of fossil bones in Haddonfield, New Jersey, more than a hundred years ago, led to a determined search of the area. Joseph Leidy, a professor of anatomy, became interested and, with his scientific background, was able to reconstruct the long-extinct reptile. For the reconstruction he had bones of the hind limbs, fore limbs, hind feet, twenty-eight vertebrae, the pelvis, a piece of the lower jaw, and nine teeth. From this material he pictured a tall, bulky dinosaur that browsed on plants and propped itself up, in kangaroo fashion, on hind legs and tail. Today, many discoveries later, scientists agree that Professor Leidy's description of Hadrosaurus was very accurate.

Fossil bones are not the only clues scientists work with. Of great help are impressions left in mud which fossilized: impressions of skin, of the form of a body, of feet.

Footprints are especially important, seeming to give action to ancient bones. They can indicate whether a dinosaur walked on two legs or on all fours, and whether it was a heavyweight or light-bodied animal.

However, footprints can be misleading unless the person examining them has a wide scientific knowledge. In the Connecticut River Valley nearly a hundred and fifty years ago, Professor Edward Hitchcock came upon some strange fossilized tracks. They greatly excited him. He believed they had been produced in prehistoric times by giant birds —birds at least twelve feet tall.

A great variety of fossilized dinosaur tracks have been discovered. They were made by the reptiles walking through mud which later hardened into stone. These footprints were part of a stream bed in Texas. *Courtesy, The American Museum of Natural History.*

The Mystery Bones

After his first discovery Professor Hitchcock continued to hunt, and he devoted the rest of his life to searching for fossil tracks. They were there—by the hundreds! Collecting the chunks of rock in which they were implanted, he gave them to Amherst College which, in time, built a museum to house the collection, where they are still on display.

Professor Hitchcock not only collected, he wrote careful descriptions of the tracks and gave his opinion about the animals that had made them. He continued to believe those having three toes were made by huge birds. Some, he felt, showed the steps of lizards, turtles, and certain other animals.

In Europe knowledge was growing about dinosaurs, but Professor Hitchcock was not aware of it; he never realized his "bird tracks" had been made by the long-vanished reptiles. Nevertheless, at his death he left behind an extremely valuable collection of dinosaur footprints.

Other dinosaur tracks have helped to bring geological fame to Connecticut. In 1966 at Rocky Hill, near Hartford, a bulldozer was excavating a site for a new building when Edward McCarthy, its operator, noticed strange three-toed prints in the sandstone under his machine. Curious, he called them to the attention of other people. As a result, scientists came and identified them as tracks called Eubrontes, made by a dinosaur that walked the earth about 180 million years ago. It was about fifteen feet long and nine feet tall, and may have weighed a ton. It walked on its hind legs. Each track was well over twelve inches in length.

A state park has now been created to protect this display of tracks, linking the world of today to the world as it was during the Age of Reptiles.

Similar footprints were discovered in New Jersey in 1968. This time the revelations were made by several high school boys after a brief news item appeared in a local paper mentioning that some fossils could be seen in an out-cropping of rock at a quarry in the town of Livingston.

Little attention was given except by a few interested boys. They began to read everything available about fossil hunting. They bought suitable tools and went to the quarry to ask permission to dig. Receiving it, they went to work.

At the quarry area, the breaking of rock had exposed many ancient layers that had been concealed by newer layers for millions of years. In them the boys soon began to find numerous footprints. Excitedly they contacted the nearby Newark Museum, and Robert Salkin, a paleontology teacher from that city, came to help them investigate.

Mr. Salkin, and later other scientists, confirmed that this was no ordinary "find." It was an important chapter in the dinosaur story.

Some of the boys turned to other interests but, for many months two of them, Anthony Lessa and Paul Olsen, spent all their spare time fossil hunting. And they were rewarded. They found a great variety of footprints—some fourteen inches in length, others made by some of the smallest dinosaurs known to science. Hundreds and hundreds of footprints!

Since that time, in 1970, there have been hopes of turning this area into another dinosaur park. To date, however, this has not become a reality.

Today the hunt continues in many parts of the world. An exciting discovery recently has been reported from western Colorado. Paleontologist James Jensen, after hear-

Paul Olsen and Anthony Lessa became enthusiastic amateur paleontologists when they found fossilized dinosaur footprints at a quarry
near their homes. *Photo by James M. Staples.*

ing from amateur rock collectors of an interesting fossil possibility, went to work on a prehistoric river bed. Months of effort produced the skeleton of a large carnivorous dinosaur and many other fossil bones. But the best was still to come—the remains of a huge four-legged reptile that had been fifty feet tall and a hundred feet from nose tip to tail tip.

It is still being worked on, and Mr. Jensen says, "I believe we are uncovering the largest dinosaur ever found on the face of the earth."

Everyone knows, of course, that finding good fossil remains—from skeletons to footprints—will never produce a living dinosaur. But the thrill of discovering new clues to the earth's past is ever challenging. There are still mysteries to be solved.

2. A Hundred and
Forty Million Years

Even in one person's lifetime it is possible to see the earth changing—and not with just man-made changes, as when woods and fields are turned into building lots and highways. In the natural course of events shore lines are washed away by pounding waves and new inlets formed. Islands can appear suddenly after volcanic action. An earthquake can greatly alter the contours of land over many miles.

If landscapes can change so much in a short time, who can picture what has happened to the earth over millions of years?

Without an understanding of fossils and rocks, even vivid imaginations would not help people reconstruct the past. But with such understanding, scientists have done brilliant work. They studied the layers of rock that make up the earth's foundation, comparing the fossils found in its different layers. They tested radioactive materials in ancient rocks, and so were able to determine their age.

After a vast number of facts had been assembled, scientists made up a calendar indicating the time involved from the earth's beginnings to the present. Then they divided these billions of years into certain time periods. There are six "eras," with each era divided into periods.

This calendar of geologic time begins in truly "dark ages"—long before there were dinosaurs; long before there were fish in the seas; before there was any animal or plant life. During the first two eras, the world was a bleak yet violent place, made up of rock, sand, and water. The only action was furnished by wind and rain storms, and the eruption of volcanoes.

Many millions of years passed before the first living organisms appeared. These were so simple and tiny they are considered neither plant nor animal. More time was needed for the development of these two forms of life.

Five hundred and fifty million years ago the third era—the Paleozoic—began, and during it, life developed in a number of interesting ways. In the waters there were soft creatures such as jellyfish, and others with spiny skins like the starfish of today. There were shellfish and "joint-footed" animals—forerunners of the lobster and other modern arthropods. But none of these creatures had backbones; they were invertebrates.

A Hundred and Forty Million Years

Dinosaurs from various time periods. In the foreground is Stegosaurus; wading in the shallow lake is Brontosaurus. Both these kinds lived millions of years before Tyrannosaurus (left center). Behind these giants are several duck-billed dinosaurs. This type roamed the earth during the time of both Stegosaurus and Tyrannosaurus. *Courtesy, The American Museum of Natural History. Painting by Robert Kane.*

Then came several spectacular changes. Certain animals came into existence whose body structure included a backbone. These vertebrates, like the invertebrates, lived in the sea. Later, some of the vertebrates developed lungs which they used, in addition to gills, for breathing.

Further development made it possible for these animals to live out of water, at least for part of their lives. They were the first amphibians.

In large, warm inland seas and small waterholes, amphibians flourished, increasing constantly in variety and numbers. Later, when reptiles came into existence, they were of less importance than the "double life" animals.

However, the reptiles' turn was coming! During the last twenty-five million years of the Paleozoic Era, enormous geologic changes took place. Great mountain ranges rose out of the earth's crust, with peaks pushing several miles toward the sky. And there was an uplifting of continental masses so that land areas increased while ocean basins deepened. A great inland sea that had covered much of North America drained away. An inland sea of India was extended northward to cover Tibet and much of China.

These and other dramatic changes were a shock to plant and animal life, and conditions that had been so ideal for amphibians no longer existed in many places. Where climate was affected—mild temperatures giving way to cold—plant life suffered severely. Some important forms, such as seed-producing ferns, completely vanished.

But with all the destruction, there were beginnings of new life and vigor in settings that were to become as perfect for reptiles as the Paleozoic "stage" had been for amphibians. A new era, the Mesozoic (often called the Age of

Reptiles) began. This was to last 140 million years, and to-day is famous, above all, for its dinosaurs.

On what sort of earth did the dinosaurs live during that long span of time? What were their advantages and their problems?

Helpfully, the world's climate grew more stable. The clouds of ash that volcanic eruptions had produced were breaking up so that the sun's warmth was again felt. Ice sheets melted. Mountain peaks wore down so that moisture-laden winds could sweep inland from the sea, bringing rain to some mid-continental deserts.

The eastern portion of North America was considerably higher above sea level than it is today. It had a warm, moist climate. In the west conditions varied because swamps and shallow seas would dry up, then rain and shifting water-ways would bring them back again.

The Mesozoic landscapes on which dinosaurs roamed were green and gorgeous. Ferns, conifers, mosses, algae, and horsetails all flourished. Even more abundant were the cycads—palmlike plants that took over the vegetation king-dom much as the dinosaurs dominated the animals. Some cycads were low-growing; they had practically no stems, but great masses of foliage. Others were as tall as trees, with stems fifty or sixty feet tall. Beautiful ginkgoes grew in profusion. Like the cycads, they took many forms, from vines and shrubs to sizable trees.

Two kinds of vegetation that, today, are taken for granted were missing from the Mesozoic landscapes: grass and hardwood trees such as maples and oaks.

In the marshy lowlands and shallow lagoons that spread over many areas, aquatic plants flourished. Here the herbivorous (plant-eating) dinosaurs could graze without danger of a food shortage. Their only problems concerned the big carnivorous (flesh-eating) dinosaurs which lurked close by, waiting for a right moment to attack and devour.

Other reptiles that shared the Mesozoic scene with the dinosaurs were the ancestors of crocodiles, turtles, lizards, and snakes. Flying reptiles were more spectacular, but the Mesozoic Era was already millions of years old before they came into existence.

The flying reptiles, named pterodactyls ("wing-finger"), varied greatly in size. There were species that grew only a few inches in length; some were monsters with a wing-spread of twenty-five feet; and there were many others in between.

An interesting "cousin" of the pterodactyls began flying over prehistoric landscapes at about the same time the reptiles took to the air. This was the oldest known bird—Archaeopteryx ("ancient wing"). It was about the size of a crow, with feathers over part of its body and along the wings. Like the pterodactyls, this earliest of birds lived for many years while dinosaurs roamed the earth. However, by the end of the Mesozoic Era, Archaeopteryx was extinct.

Insects were abundant during the Age of Reptiles—flying, creeping, and crawling among the trees and smaller plants. Some, such as dragonflies, cockroaches, ants, termites, and grasshoppers, survived to the present day, although they became smaller in size.

In the ancient seas of Mesozoic times were creatures that "out-monstered" some monster dinosaurs. They, too, were reptiles but their ancestors had turned back to life in the water after *their* ancestors had become land dwellers.

[16]

Long-necked plesiosaurs, although reptiles, spent their lives in the sea. *Courtesy, The American Museum of Natural History.*

There were ichthyosaurs ("fish lizards") from twenty to thirty feet in length, and plesiosaurs ("near lizards") with an extremely long snakelike neck and paddle-shaped limbs attached to the body by powerful muscles.

The mosasaurs ("sea lizards") were most spectacular. All were large. One, Tylosaurus, which swam through the shallow seas covering parts of western North America, surpassed many of the dinosaurs in bulk. The body was flexible and tapered off to a long, strong tail. Like the plesiosaurs it had "paddles" to aid in locomotion. Its enormous mouth was filled with daggerlike teeth. Altogether, Tylosaurus was a menace to every creature that swam in prehistoric seas.

Tylosaurus was one of the spectacular "sea lizards" living in the seas of western North America. *Courtesy, The American Museum of Natural History.*

There were marine crocodiles during Mesozoic times which approached Tylosaurus in size. However, they began to settle in the lower reaches of rivers and estuaries rather than swimming in deep, open water, and from such locations they must have seized and feasted on many an unlucky dinosaur.

The Mesozoic Era during which these many animals flourished is divided into three periods: Triassic, Jurassic, and Cretaceous. Changes took place during all of them, but through the entire era, reptiles remained outstanding. And even in the following era, when mammals surpassed them in importance, a number survived. Or they produced descendants which are still on earth today.

But the dinosaurs vanished completely.

3. The Dinosaur "Family Tree"

To be of real importance, a "family tree" must go back to its beginnings. A few generations usually do not reveal facts of great interest.

Fortunately the dinosaurs' family tree has been traced to its very roots. Although the past existence of these reptiles was discovered less than two hundred years ago, by the beginning of the twentieth century, abundant knowledge about them was shared by scientists. Some paleontologists were devoting all their efforts to finding fossils of dinosaurs and related animals. They were anxious to classify them in the way modern animals were being classified, and to trace their evolution from beginning to end. Today the family tree is clear and quite complete—documented by countless fossils found in many parts of the world.

The dinosaur story begins before the Mesozoic Era when, well over two hundred million years ago, a small, slender reptile, Youngina, lived in various areas of North Africa. In its skull were two openings, one above the other.

During early Mesozoic times Youngina, and perhaps similar reptiles, produced descendants known as thecodonts ("case tooth"). The name does not refer to the openings in the skull, but to the teeth, which were set in sockets in the jaws. Like Youngina they had deep, narrow skulls. There was an opening in the skull on either side, in front of the eye.

There was something very different about the thecodonts: The way they stood and walked was unique. From

Thecodonts, early dinosaur ancestors, were small. The kind pictured here was about four feet long. *Courtesy, The American Museum of Natural History* .

the time animals had left the water to live on land, there had been a constant development of limbs toward four-footed walking. The thecodonts found a different way to move about: They rose up on their hind limbs.

This new stance, in time, brought about drastic changes. While the hind legs grew longer and stronger, the front limbs became smaller and more like hands. They were useful for grasping rather than walking. The body, no longer supported equally at front and rear, was slung at the hip joints, and this area became the center of body motion. The hip girdle, or pelvis, grew very strong. A long tail developed which helped to balance an "unbalanced" body.

There were several types of thecodonts; their fossils have been found in South Africa and Europe. After them, the dinosaur ancestors moved on to the phytosaurs. To examine a reconstructed phytosaur is to wonder if the dinosaurs' ancestral line started to move backward at this time. The creatures walked on four legs instead of two. They looked like crocodiles and behaved much like them, spending long hours in the water, sunning themselves on river and lake banks, and snatching in their jaws any unwary animals that came near.

But although phytosaurs resemble modern crocodiles, they were not their ancestors. The phytosaurs developed, produced dinosaur descendants, and died away. Crocodiles evolved more slowly from their earliest ancestors and continued to live on into the modern world.

As mentioned in Chapter 1, there were two "groups" of dinosaurs, some having reptilian hips, others bird hips. Actually these form two distinct branches (or orders) on the family tree. They, in turn, are divided into suborders.

Phytosaurs resembled crocodiles, but were not their ancestors. Phytosaurs belong in the dinosaurs' family tree. *Courtesy, The American Museum of Natural History. Drawing by John C. Germann.*

One order includes the flesh-eating dinosaurs and plant-eating giants. In the second are armored, plated, horned, and duck-billed dinosaurs.

Here was a remarkable "family" in the animal kingdom. What happened that every last member perished? Why did not even a few small, undemanding species, or one or two of the powerful giants, survive?

There are theories that attempt to answer this question, but nobody is sure which one, if any, is correct. Possibly a combination of causes resulted in their disappearance.

One blow to the dinosaurs' well-being must have been the change that took place in world geography and weather conditions. Over much of the earth warm climates were replaced by cold, changeable weather, and plant-filled swamps disappeared. The earth shifted, and humid lowlands gave way to rolling uplands. Jungles of palm and fig trees that stayed green the year round were replaced by hard-wood forests.

As many centuries of change elapsed, the plant-eaters must have suffered starvation. And their dwindling numbers cut down the food supply of the flesh-eaters. But still there is a puzzle: Why could not a few small species whose members needed little food, survive the hardships as other reptiles, such as turtles and crocodiles, did?

Another theory concerns the "old age of the race." This indicates that animals can live out a certain span (many million years in the case of dinosaurs) and then die away simply because they have grown too old to continue.

One factor that surely must have worked against the dinosaurs was the development of mammals. These "new" animals quite possibly ate dinosaur eggs. And, having keener

Dr. Edwin Colbert, whose fossil discoveries contribute greatly to an understanding of the earth's history, explains about dinosaur ancestors to a young visitor as he shows her a phytosaur's jawbone. *Photo by James Staples.*

brains, they could outwit the dinosaurs in obtaining food. The mammals bore living young instead of producing eggs and, unlike the cold-blooded, sluggish dinosaurs, they were able to remain alert and active when the temperatures dropped.

While dinosaurs were dying away, so also went other of the great reptiles—the monsters of the sea and the ptero-dactyls of the air. As the Age of Amphibians had ended 140 million years earlier, the Age of Reptiles now came to a close. It was time for the mammals to have their age. And until humans appeared and learned to "read" fossils, the secrets of dinosaurian life were locked into the earth.

4. Youthful Fossil Hunters

Once the prehistoric existence of dinosaurs had been discovered, a number of individuals and scientific institutions set out to learn everything possible about the strange reptiles. Expeditions to far distant places were carried out, and many of them were highly successful.

As a result, popular articles and books, as well as scientific papers, about dinosaurs began to be published, and the general public became interested. Even so, collecting fossils and identifying them remained, as a rule, in the hands of experts.

This state of affairs has changed. Today a number of

amateurs enjoy fossil hunting as a hobby. Paleontology and geology are popular studies in high schools and colleges. And now a program for elementary schools in Newark, New Jersey, is making fossil hunting possible for fifth-grade girls and boys. The project is the creation of Robert Salkin, cheerfully nicknamed "Mr. Fossil" by the enthusiastic young people who learn about dinosaurs from him.

Mr. Salkin did not plan for a career as a paleontologist. He was well established as a teacher of industrial arts when a home-beautification activity changed the course of his life. He decided to make a rock garden, and among the rocks he picked up for the purpose was one on which sea shells and odd markings that looked like tiny lobster tails were imprinted. This aroused his curiosity. What were sea shells doing in an inland section of New Jersey?

He took the rock to the Newark Museum where he learned that the fossilized shells were more than three hundred million years old, the "lobster tails" had been trilobites, and the rock, many thousands of years ago had been moved from the north to the New Jersey area by a glacier.

What an exciting glimpse of prehistoric life bound up in a small piece of rock! After that Mr. Salkin looked at all rocks very carefully, and began taking college courses in paleontology and geology. His vacation trips were devoted to fossil hunting throughout the United States. He gave especially interesting finds to The American Museum of Natural History, the Newark Museum, and Princeton University, and so became acquainted with the paleontologists of these institutions.

To his surprise, he suddenly found that scientists were accepting him as belonging to their profession. His reputa-

tion grew and he began to receive calls asking that he identify footprints or other fossils that had been accidently
discovered. Still as a hobby, he gave talks about fossils to
hundreds of school and museum groups.

After ten years of such activity, Mr. Salkin had an exciting opportunity. He was able to become a full-time paleontology teacher. Federal funds under Title I, through the
Newark Board of Education, made it possible. His program
would include lectures to fifth-graders in Newark schools,
followed by the young people visiting his studio at the
Newark Museum for a fossil workshop. Then in the spring
the same groups would be taken by bus to northern New
Jersey or Pennsylvania for an actual collecting trip.

The program was an immediate success and now, several
years later, it is still flourishing. Close to ten thousand girls
and boys have gone fossil hunting with him.

A day's outing with a bus load of youthful fossil hunters
is a happy experience. Many of them talk excitedly about
"going to find a dinosaur." But, as the bus moves along busy
New Jersey highways, heading for the Delaware Water
Gap, Mr. Salkin explains the possibilities.

"Of course it's fun to think we're looking for dinosaurs,"
he says, speaking through a bullhorn so that everyone can
hear. "But the collecting grounds we're heading for today
will have fossils that actually are *older* than the dinosaurs.
Who can name some of them?"

"Trilobites."

"Crinoids."

"Brachiopods."

Answers come from different parts of the bus. Mr. Salkin acknowledges all of them.

"Right! Those invertebrates all were flourishing more than three hundred million years ago. A lot of changes took place after that before dinosaurs came along. We'll find our fossils today on a rocky mountain slope, but back when trilobites were living, the area was a large fresh-water sea.

"Right now we are close to a fine lot of dinosaur footprints. Just beyond those buildings"—Mr. Salkin continues pointing through the bus window—"more than a thousand were discovered in a quarry. They were discovered, by the way, by two high school boys who reported their find to me. We are hoping the area will become a 'dinosaur park' some day."

"Were any dinosaur bones found with the footprints?" a girl asks.

"No. And considering the great number of footprints that have been found in New Jersey, there have been few skeletons. Or even parts of skeletons," Mr. Salkin tells her. "I'll try to explain why this is so. But first, let's review what fossils are."

"Bones turned to stone."

"Impressions on rock."

"Something millions of years old."

"All right. All right," Mr. Salkin says, laughing. "Each answer is partly right. Only *partly* because it doesn't tell enough.

"Many of our most interesting discoveries *are* millions of years old. But they don't have to date that far back. Those from more than twelve thousand years ago may be considered fossils. To start, you might say that a fossil is evidence of ancient life—fossilized bones, plants, shells, molds. Even fossilized skin.

"Let's think about the bones first. When an animal dies, its bones, along with flesh and skin, usually decay and crumble. But if it dies in a location where it is quickly covered with mud or sand, the decaying process is slow. Then if conditions are right, the soft matter in the bones is replaced by minerals from the earth surrounding them. This could happen in a few thousand years, or it might take millions.

"A great many dinosaurs have been found in sandstone. But one skeleton found by Roy Chapman Andrews was composed of iron. The animal's body had been lying in water that contained a great deal of this element.

"Another type of fossil shows the natural mold of a body or shell. If a shell was enclosed in mud or sand, then dissolved, and the space it left was filled with lime or silica, this would become a fossil, shaped like the original shell.

"We're sure to find fossils of this sort on our trip today.

"Plant fossils are formed like that too. A leaf or stem leaves its impression in mud. In time minerals fill the spaces left as the hard fibers dissolved. Then the minerals become stone."

Mr. Salkin interrupts himself to again point out of the bus window, this time toward a large reservoir.

"More dinosaur evidence," he says. "But this time, only one footprint. It was found close by that water. A fossilized fish skeleton was found there too.

"But now back to our dinosaur bones, and why they don't show up very often, even where there are many footprints. It could be that the bones were too delicate to be

As fossil hunters explored this cliff, it was difficult for them to believe the dry rocks once had been a coral reef, covered with water. *Photo by James Staples.*

preserved in certain sediments. The footprints, sinking into thick mud, were more rugged. This could explain our mystery of footprints without skeletons."

A boy protests. "Dinosaur bones don't seem delicate. They looked heavy and solid when I saw them in a museum."

"Now, I'm glad you mentioned that," says Mr. Salkin. "People are likely to forget that most of the solid substance we see as part of the bones actually is rock—the rock that formed in cavities *once filled with air*. The bones of living dinosaurs, even the big ones, were delicate, possibly as delicate as in modern salamanders and other reptiles."

"Did you ever find a dinosaur skeleton in New Jersey?" a boy asks.

"No," Mr. Salkin replies. "But my very best find was of a phytosaur—which was a dinosaur ancestor—when I was fossil hunting in the northern part of the state with three boys from Newark Central High School. I gave the skull and other bones to The American Museum of Natural History, and they can be seen there today.

"The Museum paleontologists were happy to have the material and my wife was happy to have them get it," Mr. Salkin continues with a smile. "For weeks, while I was working over it and studying it, I had four hundred pounds of rock taking up space in our kitchen!

"I have made some good discoveries of dinosaur footprints, some of them when fossil hunting with friends. And I'm often called to come and identify tracks that others have discovered. You never know how important a call may turn out to be. A few years ago an engineer, Neal Resch, working on highway construction said he had noticed something interesting. We checked and found more than a hundred footprints of dinosaurs and near relatives in an area no bigger than nine feet by twenty.

"Near Princeton some school children were collecting rocks as a geology project when one of them—just about your age—came across a large area covered with well preserved dinosaur tracks. So, you just never know. . . ."

A girls asks, "When you want to hunt fossils, how do you know a good place to go?"

Mr. Salkin thinks a minute, then says, "I'm sure you know something about rocks because we've talked about them at school. In which of the three kinds—igneous, sedimentary and metamorphic—do you think fossils would most likely be found?"

It is the girl's turn to think. Then she answers hopefully, "Sedimentary."

"Right!" Mr. Salkin is pleased. "Sedimentary rocks are made up of small bits of sediment—of perhaps limestone or shales or sandstone—that have been pressed together and hardened into solid pieces. While that was happening, fossils could become part of them.

"But you can't expect any and all sedimentary rock to be hiding fossils. It used to be the best hunting grounds were places where a river had cut through, exposing old rock layers. And where other kinds of weathering, like winds and rain, cut away newer rock to show some that had been underneath for millions of years.

"Today, though, with all the digging in the earth to construct buildings and highways, there are many places being exposed that nature might never have brought into the open.

"Soon after I became interested in fossils, I learned there

were good collecting grounds in Pennsylvania, so I started looking around there and found several fine places. One of these is where we are going now. There are so many fossils of trilobites and other animals of the prehistoric seas, every one of you can find some if you look hard enough."

Many miles have been covered while Mr. Salkin talks with his young friends. And now he is able to point to the Delaware Water Gap—a great divide made in the Pocono Mountains by the Delaware River. This is where the highway leads, and soon the bus has passed from New Jersey into Pennsylvania.

There is happy news for everyone. It is time to stop for lunch! All pile out and find picnic tables where they can eat in the bright spring sunshine. Then on to the "dig" a short distance away.

Mr. Salkin gives last-minute instructions for safe and successful hunting.

"You'll soon see why I told you hammers and chisels aren't really necessary in this location," he says. "A lot of rock has been chipped loose from the cliff so you can pick up any number of pieces. And you'll find fossil imprints in many."

The hunt is on, and soon Mr. Salkin is besieged for information.

"Did you say a trilobite looks like a little lobster tail?"

"Is this a brachiopod?"

"What is this? It looks like *something!*"

Mr. Salkin identifies as many as he can. Others, he says, will be identified back at the classroom. He gives advice about keeping a few interesting specimens at home while presenting others to the school—a fossil exhibit, with labels

To Find a Dinosaur

Chisels and hammers are not always necessary in fossil collecting, but sometimes such tools are needed—by amateurs or professionals. *Photo by James Staples.*

Sometimes the young fossil hunters identified their own discoveries. . . . *Photo by James Staples.*

Sometimes they consulted with Robert Salkin, the leader of their expedition. *Photo by James Staples.*

explaining each piece, being a great attraction for any school to have.

Knapsacks and bags hold many fossil-bearing rocks when the word is passed, "All aboard the bus!"

On the way back to Newark everyone is relaxed and seems to have run out of questions. Mr. Salkin has a number of stories about fossil collecting to tell them. One they like especially because it is about a schoolgirl. Her name was Mary Anning and she lived on the coast of southern England more than a hundred years ago.

Mary helped her father hunt for fossil sea shells, which they sold as souvenirs. When she was twelve years old, Mary came upon something far more exciting than a sea shell. It was the skeleton of a huge reptile, over twenty feet long.

Mary's father brought scientists to see it. They said it had lived in the sea during the time dinosaurs were the outstanding land creatures. It was named Ichthyosaurus.

With this discovery to her credit, Mary really went after "big game" on her fossil hunts along the coast. She was very successful, and ten years after her Ichthyosaurus find, she unearthed Plesiosaurus, another extinct sea monster. Several years later she discovered the skeleton of a pterodactyl, and this was the first evidence that these flying reptiles had lived in England.

Throughout her lifetime Mary continued to sell fossils to museums of many countries. Her name became famous in the scientific world.

The bus leaves the highway, returning to busy city streets and the school which it left in the morning. Boys and girls get out, each carefully carrying fossils from the mountains of Pennsylvania. No dinosaurs this trip, but perhaps—someday—that will be the prize!

5. Railroads, Indians, and Dinosaurs

When a railroad was built across the North American continent, it made possible new economic developments in the United States. It also brought about new exploration of prehistoric life in the West. As miles of steel rails were laid across mountains and plains, they sometimes were placed side by side with dinosaur bones.

Back East, at about the same time—the latter half of the nineteenth century—some scientists were devoting themselves to the study of fossil vertebrates. Among them were Edward Cope and O. C. Marsh.

These two men were extraordinary in their determination to discover fossils, and particularly dinosaur remains. Edward Cope had begun at the age of five to study any skeletons he could find in museums near his home in Philadelphia. Through his teen years he constantly increased his knowledge of animal life, and at eighteen he wrote a scientific paper which was published and recognized as having some importance. Later he studied in universities and museums in Europe. Then, returning to America, he continued to hunt for fossils.

O. C. Marsh did not develop his strong interest in paleontology so early. For the first twenty years of his life there was only a hint of his future as a great paleontologist, and that was when he did some fossil collecting along the Erie Canal in his native New York State—probably nothing more than many another boy was doing. But, inheriting some money when he became of legal age, he turned enthusiastically to studies. For the next thirteen years he applied himself to undergraduate and graduate work.

With a degree from Yale University he, like Edward Cope, went to Europe in quest of more knowledge. He returned to the United States to become Professor of Paleontology at Yale. But he was not tied down to teaching. He would continue to be a student—in pursuit of dinosaurs and other prehistoric life.

These two men, Marsh and Cope, with their similar interests and energies, and with only a few years difference in their ages, should have been great friends. For a short time they did enjoy communicating with each other. However, feelings of jealousy developed and they became bitter rivals, each trying to outdo the other in discovering important fossils.

Both had hunted fossils out West on their own, but were back in the East when, in 1877, some tremendous fossil discoveries were reported to them. The most exciting one had been made as rails were laid for the Union Pacific Railroad. Embedded in a long ridge at Como Bluff, Wyoming, workmen had noticed huge, well-preserved bones.

Mr. Marsh was lucky. He managed to take control of this prehistoric treasure, and for some years he had a staff at work excavating bones and shipping them back to him in Connecticut. The bones came by the ton as loyal workers braved searing heat or below-zero temperatures and blinding snowstorms to find them.

Meanwhile Mr. Cope did not give up in the great "dinosaur contest." He sent his own men to the fossil territory which Mr. Marsh considered his own, and there was rather unfriendly competition between the collecting parties. But in spite of this unhappy relationship, the results were fantastic. Prehistoric giants were uncovered one after another. Brontosaurus, Stegosaurus, and Diplodocus were some of the dinosaurs.

Shortly before the discovery at Como Bluff, Mr. Cope had personally been exploring the West. With two companions he reached Helena, Montana, by stagecoach. There they found excitement that had nothing to do with fossils. General Custer's troops had just been destroyed by Chief Sitting Bull and his warriors.

When the residents of Helena learned of Cope's plans to hunt fossils, they begged them to give it up. Surely the victorious Indians roaming nearby plains and uplands would continue their killing if they saw them!

Foot and leg bones of a Tyrannosaurus being brought into the open in early days of "dinosaur hunting" in Wyoming. *Courtesy, The American Museum of Natural History.*

But Cope would not be discouraged. He and his fellow paleontologists, with a scout and cook, set up camp in the rugged country. There they spent long days clambering over rocks, dragging work materials along, digging out their discoveries, then carrying the fossils back to camp.

There was no trouble with Indians through months of collecting but, at summer's end, there was a problem. Cope was ready to pack his best discoveries and, with horse and wagon, move them to the Missouri River. There they would board a boat—the last one that would be coming along till the following spring. He expected, of course, to have help in this difficult job from the scout and cook.

But just before pack-up time, the scout caught sight of a Sioux Indian encampment, doubtless made up of Sitting Bull's warriors.

The scout and cook took little time to decide between loyalty to the fossils and their own safety. They promptly headed for civilization, with nothing heavier to carry than a blanket, and the three scientists were left with the job of guiding the wagon piled high with fossils down hazardous slopes, without attracting the attention of the Indians. Finally reaching the river, they hustled around and found a barge they could rent. They transferred the dinosaur bones to it and, with help from a horse and a long rope, they towed the fossils to the boat landing.

Following this exciting expedition, Cope turned his attention to the discoveries at the Como Bluff area. But some years later he returned to the Sioux country where he was sure he could find skeletons of duck-billed dinosaurs. The Indians understood he was not there to fight them. Nevertheless they were very opposed to his fossil hunting.

Huge pieces of dinosaur bones were found lying in the open at Bone Cabin Quarry, Wyoming. Here some are shown being "packaged" for shipment. *Courtesy, The American Museum of Natural History.*

The Indians' objections were because of superstitions. They believed that in ancient times huge serpents had burrowed into the earth and then had been killed with bolts of lightning by the Great Spirit. And the bones imbedded in the rocks were skeletons of these ghostly reptiles. The Indians feared them and did not want them to be disturbed.

However, Cope managed to carry out his plans, and collected not only a fine duck-billed dinosaur, but other well-preserved skeletons. The trip was a highly successful one.

In 1898 a team of young men—members of the department of vertebrate paleontology at the American Museum of Natural History—went West to further explore Como Bluff. They soon discovered the best of the dinosaur skeletons had already been "harvested" from the area. More years of weathering might again make the Bluff good collecting grounds; meanwhile they would look elsewhere.

Making their way westward over miles of rocky terrain, they came to the Medicine Bow anticline, and there found an astounding sight. Huge pieces of dinosaur bones lying in the open and covering a hillside! They had been weathered out of the ridge and were just lying there, like so many chunks of ordinary rock.

Then the explorers saw a cabin, obviously built at some time by a sheep herder—a cabin constructed entirely of dinosaur bones. Not surprisingly, they named it "Bone Cabin" and the collecting area became "Bone Cabin Quarry."

The quarry would have deserved a variety of interesting names such as Dinosaur Treasure or Great Dinosaur Dig. After the first summer's work, more than sixty thousand pounds of fossils, filling two freight cars, were shipped to the museum in New York. And for the following seven

Late in the nineteenth century, railroads were new in the West. But the Union Pacific was ready to transport dinosaur bones when needed. Here fossils are being loaded on freight cars at Medicine Bow, Wyoming. The year was 1898. *Courtesy, The American Museum of Natural History.*

summers, paleontologists returned to it and to areas close by. Each year their mission was highly successful. Bones of prehistoric giants were collected in such quantities that scientists were not the only people to be fascinated. The interest of the general public was captured, and dinosaurs were brought from an unknown prehistoric past to become a part of the modern world.

6. Dinosaur National Monument

"At last, in the top of the ledge . . . I saw eight of the tail bones of a Brontosaurus in exact position."

These words, written in a diary by Earl Douglass on August 17, 1909, marked the real beginning of a project that would be carried on for fifteen years, and would eventually bring into existence the Dinosaur National Monument in Utah—said to be the world's greatest store of fossil bones.

Mr. Douglass had been exploring the area, in the rugged ridges of Split Mountain, for months. Some years earlier a scientist from The American Museum of Natural History had reported that the prospects for finding dinosaurs there were good. However, no one acted on the suggestion until 1908 when Mr. Douglass, with the director of the Carnegie Museum of Pittsburgh, went to have a look. They found some good fossils, encouraging enough so that the following summer Douglass returned for a more thorough search. And that was when he "struck"—not gold, but dinosaurs!

Besides the Brontosaurus mentioned in the diary, there would be "mined" from this prehistoric quarry Stegosaurus, Diplodocus, and numerous other dinosaurs, large and small flesh-eaters and plant-eaters. In some cases the fossil bones were concentrated and confusingly intermingled. In others, skeletons were secured in position so that no imagination was needed to restore them to the form they had as living animals.

Fortunately Earl Douglass was a man of tremendous enthusiasm and dedication. After the excitement of his discovery, noted on that long-ago August day, there was no returning to a normal life for him. He sent word about the importance of the area to Andrew Carnegie, whose money had made possible the Carnegie Museum, and began plans for a full-scale operation.

Mr. Douglass had a wife and year-old baby back East. He asked Mrs. Douglass to come out to join him. He would build a home close to the quarry because the nearest town was twenty miles away and he did not want to spend valuable time "commuting" on horseback.

Mrs. Douglass arrived with the baby, but for the first winter they had to live in a primitive shelter—canvas over wooden frames, with an iron stove as the complete heating system. This with temperatures sometimes going below zero! A sheepherder's wagon served as an office for Douglass and as sleeping quarters for his three assistants.

However, by the following summer the family had comfortable quarters in the rocky wilderness. They had built a five-room log cabin and a small dam across a gully so that ground water would be captured to serve them. They had a vegetable garden, a cow, and some chickens. Domestic life went along smoothly while Douglass gave undivided attention to the dinosaurs.

Funds furnished by Mr. Carnegie made it possible for him to employ helpers, and soon a road was built from his cabin to the discovery site. All kinds of tools were bought and a forge set up.

The following summer Douglass and his workmen had cut deep into the sandstone ridge an excavation more than a hundred feet long. They laid rails along its floor on which small mine cars could run and haul away the dirt and rock in which no fossils were embedded. This debris was pushed along the rails to the edge of a cliff where it could be dumped out of the way.

The excavation was a gigantic job because of the position of the rock layers in which the bones were entombed: The layers, instead of being in orderly position, one below the other, each layer older than the one settled on top of it, were pushed up at a sharp angle. This had happened as the result of the great earth movements that thrust the Rocky Mountains into existence.

So now the problem for the paleontologist was not to work downward, gradually cutting hidden fossils free. He had to dig away layers of rock *to the side* of the layer that held fossils.

"Snaking" fossils down a rugged path from the dinosaur quarry that was to become part of the great Dinosaur National Monument in Utah. *Courtesy, The American Museum of Natural History.*

Fossils still are being uncovered at the Dinosaur National Monument, with the aid of power tools and other modern equipment. A shelter erected over the working area protects ancient bones as they are uncovered. *Photo by James Staples.*

Douglass and his staff worked unceasingly. They broke rock with carefully placed charges of dynamite, used hard drills and crowbars to clear away the loosened pieces, and went on to more delicate work with hammer and chisel. As they released bones, along with any rock that still surrounded them, they wrapped them in protective strips of burlap that had been dipped in flour paste. (At a later date, plaster of paris was used instead of flour.) These heavy burdens were then lowered by rope to a "skid," which a team of mules would cautiously pull down a trail to the bottom of the gulch.

Still the fossils were far from their destination—the Carnegie Museum. They had to be packed in boxes and transported to a railroad more than sixty miles away. The trips were accomplished with high-wheeled freight wagons, each pulled by four-horse teams over rutted roads.

As the years of collecting continued, amazement grew over the variety of dinosaurs being revealed. Mr. Douglass felt there had to be an explanation as to why so many different types were concentrated in one relatively small locality. He carefully studied the sandstone rocks and saw from their coarse, granular texture that waters had once swirled about this area. Undoubtedly a river flowing through the swamplands of prehistoric times had carried along the carcass of many a dead animal. When these reached a sandbar, the bodies settled, and soon were buried in soft mud and sand. The great dinosaur quarry was a dramatic reminder that long ago the dry, rocky cliffs of Utah had been a low-lying, semi-tropical land.

Not only the Carnegie Museum benefited from the treas-

Dinosaur National Monument

At Dinosaur National Monument some bones, after being worked out of the rock just enough to be seen clearly, are left in place. Visitors then may examine them in the position in which they lay for millions of years. *Photo by James Staples.*

ures of this tremendous dinosaur dig. After Douglass had excavated three hundred specimens (a number of which were in good enough condition for the skeletons to be mounted) the University of Utah and the United States National Museum sent collecting parties there and they were rewarded with discoveries of their own.

Early in his work Douglass had suggested placing the area under government protection so that it would be a heritage for future generations. A number of obstacles had to be overcome but finally, in 1915, under the Antiquities Act (designed to safeguard and preserve objects and areas of significant scientific or historic interest), the quarry and eighty acres of surrounding land were declared a National Monument. A short time after, it was included in the National Parks System.

Nearly forty years passed, however, before plans to make it a spectacular exhibition for tourists became realities. The reserved land was increased many times. A large "face" on a rocky cliff was cleared sufficiently for its dinosaur bones to be clearly visible. Then a building was constructed to enclose the face, protecting it from weathering. And still work continues, so that a feeling of life is given to this remarkable prehistoric scene.

7. Tyrannosaurus and Other Giants

A paleontologist can find the smallest dinosaur remains as interesting, or even more interesting, than a giant because it may prove to be an important clue in solving mysteries of prehistoric life. However, most people prefer to see very big dinosaur skeletons—if possible, weird in shape and features. And fortunately museums are able to exhibit a splendid variety of such monsters.

Tyrannosaurus rex is a favorite "spectacular." His name tells the story: *Tyranno* ("tyrant"), *sauros* ("lizard"), *rex* ("king"). King of the tyrant lizards.

Artist and paleontologists combined their skills and knowledge to produce this prehistoric scene—a confrontation between Tyranno-saurus and Triceratops. *Courtesy, The American Museum of Natural History. Painting by Charles R. Knight.*

Everything about Tyrannosaurus was big and strong. With a weight of several tons, he stood and walked on massive hind legs, with his head nineteen or twenty feet above the ground. From nose to tail tip was fifty feet, and his head was of suitable size for his enormous body. The jaws were four feet in length, the teeth six inches long and dagger-like. Though his front limbs were short, they were equipped with large, iron-strong claws. They could easily tear other dinosaurs to bits.

Another spectacular dinosaur was Trachodon—more popularly known as the duck-billed dinosaur. However, in spite of his size—about thirty feet in length—he was helpless when attacked by Tyrannosaurus. The duck-billed dinosaurs had no defensive armor, and practically no fighting equipment. A kick with a hind foot or a lashing out with the long tail were their only ways to discourage an attacker.

A duck-bill did have amazing teeth. Two thousand of them filled his jaws, and as old ones wore down and fell out, new teeth grew. Though these teeth were excellent for chewing vegetation, they were useless in fighting. None were at the front of the mouth; they were lined up in neat rows at either side of the jaws. There they would tear and mash the quantities of water plants which the duck-bill scooped up with his broad, flat bill.

Duck-bills must have been good swimmers. Their front feet were webbed. With these, and with mighty sweeps of the tail, they could move easily through water, going from one feeding ground to another. This ability was their best protection from Tyrannosaurus whose activities were confined to dry land. He needed something very solid under his giant feet!

Numerous skeletons of duck-billed dinosaurs have been discovered, as well as pieces of their fossilized skin. Reconstructing their image is simplified by these remains. *Courtesy, The American Museum of Natural History. Painting by Charles R. Knight.*

The fossil record of the trachodons is unique. More of their skeletons have been discovered than of any other large dinosaur. Also, a number of specimens were found with skin impressions overlying much of the animal. One of these is considered a mummy because skin so completely clothes the body.

Brontosaurus, like the duck-bills, found his food in the water, but he was not designed for swimming. With a length of about eighty feet, and weighing some forty tons, he plodded around in shallow lakes, swamps, and rivers. Though his legs were huge, their joints were not strong; the water doubtless helped support the weight of his body.

Brontosaurus ("thunder lizard") was given his name because of his tremendous size, but he was a gentle giant. His head was incredibly small for the big body. And his mouth was small, even for so small a head. His teeth were not sharp. Altogether, he was completely helpless when attacked by a hungry flesh-eater. Weighing almost as much as a dozen elephants, he had less power than a single one. When threatened, his only hope of safety was to escape into water where an enemy such as Allosaurus could not follow.

Brontosaurus had some close relatives, built much as he was. One was Diplodocus, more slender in body, but longer —in fact, with his extraordinary, whip-like tail, he was the longest of all dinosaurs. Another "cousin" was Brachiosaurus, whose body was even heavier than that of the thunder lizard.

Allosaurus flourished during the same period as Brontosaurus. Like Tyrannosaurus (who lived at a later time) Allosaurus walked on his two hind legs. His front limbs were small but ended in vicious hooked claws.

Interesting work was done by paleontologists who found a skeleton of Brontosaurus which showed toothmarks on many parts of the backbone. Nearby was the skeleton of an Allosaurus. His teeth were compared with the marks on the Brontosaurus bones, and they fitted exactly!

Some broken teeth of Allosaurus also were discovered mixed with the Brontosaurus bones. From these clues a clear picture could be constructed of a giant's violent death many millions of years ago.

Not all plant-eating dinosaurs were helpless. Some of them wore protective armor. Stegosaurus was a striking example of this type. Though not very large—about fifteen feet long—he looked impressive with a series of upright, triangular bone plates running down the middle of his back. At the tip of his heavy tail were four big spikes. Here was an effective weapon when swung at an attacker.

Fortunately for Stegosaurus he had a much enlarged spinal cord in his hips—a nerve center that controlled the movements of his hind limbs and the powerful tail. He had need of this instinctive aid to survival, for his brain was no larger than a walnut. *Thinking* about avoiding danger would surely have been beyond his ability.

Ankylosaurus, a short, squat dinosaur, also grew bone plates, but these did not stand on end. They lay flat on the body and head, forming an effective suit of armor. As with Stegosaurus, the tail served as a weapon. It was heavy, stiff, and ended in a huge mass of bone.

The Ceratopsians were the last of all dinosaurs to develop before the Age of Reptiles gave way to the Age of Mammals. The Ceratopsians had horns.

At first there was Protoceratops ("first horn face"). Actually this small dinosaur, which grew no longer than five or six feet, had only the suggestion of a horn on his nose. But other dinosaurs did not have even that. He also had a unique parrot-like beak, formed by the front of his muzzle and jaws.

Protoceratops lived in the area that today is the Gobi Desert of Asia. But his descendants wandered far from this habitat. Eventually some came to North America, crossing on a land bridge that stretched from Asia. Here they flour-

Monoclonius, a mighty horned dinosaur that lived in the area of Alberta, Canada. *Courtesy, The American Museum of Natural History. Painting by Charles R. Knight.*

ished, and in time mighty Triceratops ("three-horn face") evolved.

The skull alone of Triceratops was larger than the entire body of his early ancestors. It was about eight feet long, about half of it being an enormous bone frill. In place of the little bump that earlier had perched on the nose of Protoceratops, there was now a stout horn, and two other horns projected from over the eyes.

Triceratops' heavy head was attached to the backbone by a strong ball-and-socket joint, and he had tremendous neck and leg muscles. With this structure the great beast was capable of doing the near-impossible—that is, challenging the might of Tyrannosaurus. With head lowered he could lunge at the tall, upright "tyrant," and pierce his flesh with those sharp horns.

A number of scientists have gained fame in connection with the dinosaurs they discovered. Tyrannosaurus and other giants became a "trademark" of Barnum Brown who, for sixty-six years, was a scientist on the staff of The American Museum of Natural History.

Dr. Brown found a skull of Triceratops while he was still a college student. And only a few years later, on an expedition for the American Museum, he unearthed some bones of Tyrannosaurus. This was exciting, but far from satisfactory to him. He wanted a *complete* Tyrannosaurus skeleton. And he finally found one, in the Bad Lands of Montana.

8. From the Bad Lands to Red Deer River

When Barnum Brown set out to find dinosaur fossils in the "Wild West" of 1902, he and his companions walked from a railroad more than 130 miles in five days over rugged, inhospitable country. By then they reached the Bad Lands of Montana which, he had been told, might be worth a paleontologist's attention.

The Badlands were beautiful, with orange, yellow, and red rocky cliffs, but most uncomfortable for camping. They had been given their name because they seemed good for nothing but discomfort. And for fossil treasure, as it turned out!

Dr. Brown lost no time beginning investigations. In a small stream, called Hell Creek, next to which camp was set up, there were a number of large, rounded pieces of sandstone. The scientists checked where these had come from, tracing them up a long, rocky slope. Suddenly the prize lay before them—a complete skeleton of Tyrannosaurus, still holding the pose in which it had fallen at death.

The first step in freeing the giant's bones from the earth was easy—nothing more than brushing away loose surface

This area in Montana, near a small stream called Hell Creek, looked unexciting—until the complete skeleton of a Tyrannosaurus was found there. *Courtesy, The American Museum of Natural History.*

earth and stones. But as the workers continued, they found the sandstone as hard as iron. Dynamite and heavy tools were then used to work around the bones until a hole twenty-five feet deep, thirty feet long and twenty feet wide had been made.

With this great cavity, it was possible to cut the iron-like sandstone containing the fossils into blocks. Some were huge; one weighed more than four thousand pounds. A team of four horses was needed to pull it, in a wagon, to the railroad.

Two summers of hard work were carried on before the entire skeleton of this Tyrannosaurus reached the American Museum, where it was prepared for exhibition.

For several more years the Bad Lands claimed Dr. Brown's attention, during which he found another Tyrannosaurus as well as skeletons of duck-billed dinosaurs. After that, he decided to explore other territories.

His choice of a new location was far to the north, along the steep banks of the Red Deer River in Alberta, Canada. He was not the first to explore the area, for several geologists had been there and had reported seeing an extraordinary number of fossils along the river.

Dr. Brown soon demonstrated his original touch in the pursuit of fossils. Instead of using an ordinary boat to navigate the river, he had a very special one constructed. It was flat-bottomed and large—large enough to transport both fossil hunters and the fossils they collected. Its only steering equipment was a long "sweep" at each end; it was maneuvered like an old barge. This might have been completely satisfactory if the river had been slow-moving at all times. But in some stretches the current was swift,

The pelvis, part of a large Tyrannosaurus skeleton, is being hoisted into a crate. *Courtesy, The American Museum of Natural History.*

and every now and then rapids presented a serious problem.

Nevertheless, in time the floating camp reached quiet waters, and Dr. Brown could give full attention to the cliffs on either side of the river where fossils were surely waiting to be found. He knew that Red Deer River was a young water course, but it had cut down through hundreds of feet of rock. Thus had been formed the deep canyon which his keen and practiced eyes scanned. Whenever a spot looked promising, he left the boat and scrambled up the cliff to investigate.

Barnum Brown comes ashore from his floating camp on Red Deer River to work on a dinosaur skeleton. *Courtesy, The American Museum of Natural History.*

The bones of dinosaur after dinosaur were found, some of them quite spectacular. One was a crested dinosaur, Saurolophus, closely related to the Trachodon. On the back of its head was a great bone crest; in life this had supported a lobe of skin such as decorates some lizards. It was thirty-two feet long and stood seventeen feet high. The remains of hundreds of individuals were found in one fairly small area.

Another crested dinosaur discovered by Dr. Brown was especially interesting because, along with the bones, were some clear skin impressions.

Many other fossils appeared in the rocky gorge as the unusual barge cruised along Red Deer River. By the end of the summer its storage space was piled high with the remains of prehistoric animals. Such success called for further expeditions, and the following year Dr. Brown returned for more collecting. Again he was most successful, and started planning future work. But by then he had competition!

Canadians had been interested and impressed by the prehistoric life of their country as it was being revealed by Dr. Brown. Then suddenly protests began. Why should this scientist be carrying their fossils back to the United States, with Canada doing nothing about making collections of its own?

The Geological Survey of Canada, which had given Dr. Brown permission to collect, did not withdraw its consent to his work. Instead they decided that Canadian scientists should "hunt dinosaurs" on their own.

Fortunately the services of a family team were available. Charles H. Sternberg, a noted paleontologist who had collected dinosaur fossils in the United States, had three sons—all of whom shared his interest and skills. And when asked to do so, the family organized without delay to explore the cliffs of Red Deer River.

The Sternbergs set up a camp on land, near the spot at which Dr. Brown began his first cruise. They had a field wagon in which fossils could be transported, and an oversized rowboat from which they could search the faces of the cliffs.

The following summer, however, they adopted the idea of camping on the river instead of beside it. Besides a very large barge with two tents on its deck, the Sternbergs had a motor boat which could tow the flat-bottom, and it also could be used for running errands. Again they made use of their very large rowboat.

Of course there was keen rivalry between the two groups of explorers as, almost side by side, they hunted dinosaurs. But it was carried on with good will. This might have been hard to achieve if fossils had been scarce. Happily, there was a wealth of fossils, and the Canadian museums in Ottawa and Toronto and the exhibits of the American Museum in New York, were all greatly enriched by the collecting done along Red Deer River.

Charles Sternberg and his sons found some excellent duck-billed dinosaurs, an armored species, a horned species, and other, varied types. Like Dr. Brown, they were fortunate enough to discover skeletons on which the animal's skin had become fossilized along with its bones.

Barnum Brown returned to this great natural storehouse of fossils summer after summer for six years until 1915. The Sternbergs ended their work as a team in the area shortly after. However, two of the brothers continued their dedication to the project. For the remainder of their lives they went back again and again in search of pre-historic treasure, and they devoted themselves, as well, to research concerning their discoveries and having their findings published.

9. The Treasure of Central Asia

By 1923 it might seem that, among the general public, excitement over dinosaurs would have quieted down. Remains of the ancient reptiles had been found north, south, east, and west on the North American continent. And they were well known in Europe. Of course there were still mysteries about them, but the weird animals had been accepted—established as part of the earth's history.

However, in that year a dramatic discovery turned all eyes toward dinosaur hunting. In the remote, formidable desert of Asia, known as the Gobi, dinosaur eggs were found.

Until that time, one of the mysteries of prehistoric life was: How did dinosaurs produce their young? Did females give birth to living babies or did they lay eggs? With modern reptiles both types of reproductions prevail. So, for lack of evidence, scientists could only guess about these reptiles of the past.

Then came the revelation of dinosaur eggs.

To appreciate fully the drama of this discovery, it is necessary to know the story behind a group of American scientists who undertook a great project in a far-off, desolate part of Asia.

As first planned, the expedition was not intending to look for dinosaur remains. Its purpose was to seek evidence about the origin of mankind and some of the earth's earliest mammals.

Roy Chapman Andrews, a young and vigorous scientist on the staff of The American Museum of Natural History, was to be its leader. And from the moment the idea was suggested to him, he began to plan for exploring on a grand scale.

The obstacles were tremendous. The Gobi stretched for two thousand miles through the heart of Mongolia. Its climate—fiercely hot most of the short summer, bitterly cold in winter—left a very brief time in which men could survive to work. The few explorers who had tried to investigate its interior had returned to civilization with nothing more than descriptions of their sufferings.

Its sparse vegetation consisted of thorny bushes, clumps of hard, sharp grass, and sage brush. The only living animals were wolves, wild ass, and gazelle. Some Mongolian natives were known to roam across the gravel-covered

Roy Chapman Andrews (standing) goes to greet the camel caravan, which is bringing supplies for his expedition in Mongolia. *Courtesy, The American Museum of Natural History.*

earth, but they were not likely to be friendly to strangers. They were bandits.

Until 1922 camels were the only means of transportation that had been used on this desolate land. But Dr. Andrews had other ideas. He would use cars—although this was long before the rough-riding Jeep had been invented.

Advisors tried to persuade him that such a plan would never work. However he persisted. By using motorized transportation, he reasoned, the scientists would have time and energy to hunt for fossils. Otherwise the short span in which temperatures would allow them to survive would fly by without anything important being accomplished.

Dr. Andrews realized that cars could not be depended on to carry all the necessary heavy supplies. Therefore a camel caravan, made up of more than a hundred animals, would bring food, gasoline and oil along carefully planned routes. And at points mapped out in advance, at certain specified times, the cars would meet the camels. At these get-togethers enough supplies would be given the explorers to last till the next meeting, and any fossils collected would be transferred to camel-back.

With high hopes, courage, and determination, the expedition set out in the spring of 1922. Altogether there were forty men, some of them among the world's outstanding scientists.

Once in China, they began the steep drive, on deeply rutted roads, toward the Great Wall. When they finally passed through a narrow gateway in the wall, the Gobi —their challenge—spread out before them.

Three days of hard riding passed before the paleontol-

Discovering dinosaur eggs was an outstanding achievement of the Central Asiatic Expeditions. Here Dr. Andrews and fellow workers admire a nest that held an "even dozen." *Courtesy, The American Museum of Natural History.*

ogists reached an area they thought looked promising for fossils. Then even before tents were pitched, some of the men started hunting. Soon a small collection of fossil bones had been made, and despite their long, hard hours of travel, everyone was too excited for much sleep.

By the next day's sunrise all were ready for action. Dr. Walter Granger, another American Museum scientist (years before he had been responsible for remarkable dinosaur discoveries in Wyoming) and others started roaming the area with whiskbrooms, brushes, and chisels. Dr. Andrews, however, applied himself to setting out traps for small mammals. This expedition, he kept in mind, was to investigate all phases of life in the Asiatic desert.

But the trap-setting had barely begun when he was interrupted and asked to come to the crest of a ridge, where he found Dr. Granger carefully brushing the coarse sand. Under his brush, encased in rock, was a large, well-preserved bone. The scientists looked at it with excitement and, almost, disbelief. It was part of the skeleton of a reptile, and the reptile, they felt sure, had been a dinosaur.

Dinosaurs. That was a magic word to the men seeking to piece together the story of the earth. Their enthusiasm was so great it raced through the camp, and soon everyone from Dr. Andrews to the Chinese cooks and Mongolian guides were searching the fossil fields from morning till dark.

The weeks passed much too quickly, as more and more dinosaur bones were found. The geologists of the party decided that the area, something like seventy-five million years before, had been a great lake. Apparently there had been a swirl of water that carried the bodies of dead animals into a backwash. There the whirlpool lost its grip on them and they sank to the bottom of the lake. In time the bones sank into the mud and eventually changed to stone.

This theory was based, in part, on the fact that many duck-billed dinosaurs were among the skeletons found; they would have been browsing on plants in the lake. And there were remains, also, of some flesh-eating species. These carnivorous dinosaurs doubtless attacked the duck-bills, and many a struggle must have taken place with both contestants finally being drowned.

Of course, as Dr. Andrews and his companions looked around them, they saw no sign of the lake or tropical vegetation. Only sand, gravel, thorny plants—and bones —to tell of a far-distant age.

The expedition members would have liked to stay on and on. But they knew that to remain beyond September would be risking disaster. The summer's work had been successful: besides dinosaur and other fossil bones, a good collection of mammals and plants had been made. Clearly it was time to leave for home.

Their adventures were not over, however. As the cars slowly moved back toward the Great Wall, a stop was made to search for water. Soon the men found not only a well but an extraordinary dinosaur "graveyard."

The first fossil discovery was a bleached-out white skull, eight inches long, resting on a red sandstone cliff. Nearby was a huge basin that had been scooped out of the plain by weathering. Its over-all color was pink but at sunset, purple and red tones made it a riot of color. In the midst of which gleamed bits of white fossil bones!

The men named it the Flaming Cliffs, and vowed to return there the following summer. Then they moved on their way. This was fortunate, for only two days later a blizzard raged over the region.

Back at the American Museum studies of the fossils disclosed that one skull found at the Flaming Cliffs belonged to an ancestor of the monstrous three-horned Triceratops of North America. The smaller "horned" dinosaur (with really only a bump on its nose), was named Protoceratops. The paleontologists waited impatiently for the next summer when they could learn more about this species.

In 1923 the expedition again set out over the parched desert trail, managing to retrace the tracks their cars had made ten months earlier. It was midsummer when they reached the Flaming Cliffs, and for more than a month they concentrated on this one area.

There were Protoceratops bones in abundance. Twelve skeletons and seventy-five skulls! And they were not duplicates of each other. Some were the remains of babies only a few inches long, on which the "frill" over the neck had not yet begun to show. In one specimen of an adult, every bone was in place, from the hooked "beak" to the end of the tail. It seemed the animal must have been about to crawl forward when overtaken by death, and was then quickly covered with sand.

But all these discoveries were overshadowed by one made shortly after the expedition's arrival at the Flaming Cliffs. Dinosaur *eggs*.

The first time there were only three, lying on a small rock ledge. Obviously they had broken out of crumbling

Protoceratops, shown hatching from its egg—in a museum exhibit. This dinosaur is especially well known because some fossilized eggs were discovered that contained babies in various stages of development. *Courtesy, The American Museum of Natural History.*

sandstone just above. Coming into view, among the broken sandstone, were several more.

When loose sediment had been brushed away, in preparation for cutting out a large piece of rock that contained the eggs, another fossil was seen. It was the skeleton of a small dinosaur, unknown up to that time. Later it was named Oviraptor—"egg stealer," for apparently sucking eggs had furnished its nourishment. And a windstorm had buried this individual with sand just as it was closing in on a meal.

Eggs and more eggs were discovered at the Flaming Cliffs, and many blocks of sandstone were shipped to New York. There, in the American Museum laboratories, not only was stone chipped away, but so were the cracked shells of some of the eggs. And inside were revealed the skeletons of baby dinosaurs that had been ready to hatch when the forces of nature made them into fossil exhibits for future ages.

No wonder the attention of the world's scientists and countless non-scientists, turned toward dinosaurs! They wondered: If small dinosaurs laid eggs about eight inches long, how large would a Brontosaurus egg be? Did the female dinosaur sit on her eggs to hatch them? Many questions were asked, some of which could be answered while others required further study.

During the 1923 season twenty-five eggs were found at the Flaming Cliffs. Two years later the Central Asiatic Expeditions returned to find that new weathering had exposed many more fossils. Among them were more dinosaur eggs, including one nest of a dozen and another nest of fourteen eggs, neatly laid in a circle. One member of the expedition picked up seven hundred and fifty pieces of dinosaur egg shell in a single afternoon.

The eggs apparently had been laid in a shallow hole, dug out of sand. The female dinosaur would then scratch a thin layer of sand over them, and leave them to be warmed by the sun until ready for hatching.

However, a windstorm could quickly churn and blow the sand into great heaps. If such a pile settled on top of a nest, the eggs would lose the sun's warmth. Instead of hatching, therefore, they would lie underground in a state of arrested development.

As the sand over them grew increasingly heavy, the shells cracked, allowing their liquid to run out, and grains of sand, seeping in through the cracks, replaced the liquid. For this reason the eggs did not lose their shape. And with the passing of time, eggs and the sand around them, hardened into solid rock.

Clearly the heart of Mongolia was a magnificent exploring ground for prehistoric treasure. The Central Asiatic Expeditions returned there in 1925, and in 1928 and 1930 the explorers again went to Asia, although they were not permitted to go to their favorite collecting sites. After that, political changes and military conflicts meant an end to expeditions from the Western world.

However, with the end of World War II, Russian paleontologists turned their attention to dinosaur hunting, and in 1946 they were able to take up exploring in Mongolia where Dr. Andrews and his companions had left off. But instead of heavy motor cars for scouting, they had Jeeps; instead of camels for hauling their "back-up" supplies, they used powerful trucks. Naturally they were able to travel faster, and they had the benefit of facts learned by the Central Asiatic Expeditions.

The Russian expedition visited some of the territory that had been covered before. Especially Protoceratops country! There the scientists discovered more skeletons and more eggs which obviously had been brought into view by weathering in the more than twenty years that had passed between expeditions.

Later they turned their attention to southwestern Mongolia, and there they found a fabulously rich "bone yard." Among the bones were remains of dinosaur giants—some like the huge duck-billed species and Tyrannosaurus of North America. There were smaller types as well, and the medium-sized "ostrich dinosaur," already well known in the Western Hemisphere. Altogether 120 tons of fossil bones were sent back to Moscow to be studied and exhibited.

Since then other dinosaur hunts have been carried on in Mongolia. In 1964 Polish and Mongolian scientists organized an expedition to explore the great desert where they, also, made a fine collection of skeletons: Tyrannosaurus, and duck-billed and armored dinosaurs.

With each discovery in Asia of extinct animals that were similar to extinct animals of North America, the link between these two continents became closer. Scientists had ever-mounting evidence that once upon a time dinosaurs and other creatures had wandered freely from one hemisphere to another.

10. Early to Late in Dinosaur History

North America and Asia are not the only continents whose backgrounds are linked by dinosaurs. Over many years discoveries in Africa, South America, and Australia revealed that "matching" prehistoric reptiles had been distributed over these three continents. And recently paleontologists in Antarctica found that even this continent, frozen as it is today, was once the home of reptiles and amphibians such as those which flourished near the equator.

As a result of fossil discoveries and much study, geologists have changed their thinking about the background of the continents. For a long time the similarity of prehistoric animals on the various land masses had been explained by "land bridges" such as the Isthmus of Panama (between North America and South America), the Bering Straits (between North America and Asia), and the territory linking Africa with lands to the north.

However, there was another theory. It stated that two hundred million years ago, South America, the Antarctic, Africa, Australia, and India formed one gigantic continent. It was given the name Gondwana land. The theory further suggested that Gondwana land eventually split into five major divisions, and these areas drifted away from each other until they were separated by large bodies of water.

For the most part, the "Gondwana land theory" was not taken very seriously. But during the past decade, a great amount of data gathered by scientists seemed to prove that Gondwana land really had existed. And fossils, discovered very recently in Antarctica, gave final, convincing proof of the long-vanished continent.

It is because of their desire to comprehend the earth's history that scientists ponder so diligently over fossil discoveries—small or large.

Some of the most interesting small dinosaurs were found in southern Germany about seventy years ago. Their discoverer was Friedrich von Huene. He was a college student when fossils first caught his attention. His interest in vertebrate paleontology became broad, but it was the beginnings of the dinosaur family that especially interested him.

After years of work in Europe, Professor von Huene was invited to South America to study a huge collection of dinosaur bones that had been collected and stored in the museum of La Plata.

Early to Late in Dinosaur History

Not surprisingly, he accepted the invitation and was soon in Argentina. Bones had been gathered from a number of different localities, so he went on field trips to see, first hand, the areas in which they had been found.

Many of the bones were of giants from the Cretaceous period. But on a later trip to South America, he went to Brazil where he could explore rocks formed in the Triassic, when dinosaurs were new to the world. He did not find an abundance of the prehistoric reptiles he sought, but discovered some of their ancestors, and one very small dinosaur —one of the earliest.

So Professor von Huene felt satisfied that South America had been home to dinosaurs from first to last, right through

Tools of the dinosaur hunter in New Mexico. Often such simple implements are all that are needed to uncover an important fossil. *Courtesy, The American Museum of Natural History.*

the Mesozoic Era. Meanwhile the same story was being revealed in South Africa where early dinosaurs and others were being brought to light.

In North America one rather mysterious species had been discovered back in the days of Edward Cope. An assistant working for Mr. Cope in New Mexico had found a jumbled mass of reptile bones which he shipped back East to his employer, noting that they were "small and tender," and belonged either to the Triassic or Jurassic period. Mr. Cope agreed. He sorted the bones and arranged them as best he could. And he named the dinosaur they represented Coelophysis.

Years passed, and numerous important dinosaur discoveries were made in many parts of the world. But little Coelophysis remained hidden from the searching eyes of the paleontologists. Since the pioneer days when Mr. Cope named it, only an occasional bit of bone was found that could have belonged to the species. Would this "early one" always remain a shadowy figure among relatives that were resurrected over and over again?

Finally a break-through came. Dr. Edwin Colbert, Curator of Vertebrate Paleontology at The American Museum of Natural History, decided to explore along the Arroyo Seco in New Mexico, where rocks formed during the Triassic period were abundant.

Dr. Colbert and his companions covered miles of beautiful but arid territory in a Jeep, searching for cliffs that seemed to promise fossils. Then, with an area chosen, they spent countless hours searching up and down the jagged slopes.

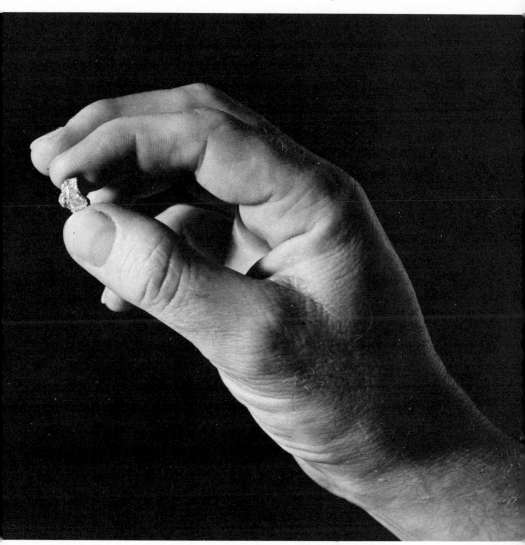

This fragment of a claw was an exciting discovery for Dr. Edwin
Colbert in New Mexico. It had belonged to Coelophysis, one of the
earliest of dinosaurs. *Courtesy, The American Museum of Natural
History.*

[89]

Success did not come at once. One day had been particularly fruitless for Dr. Colbert, and George Whitaker, his fellow explorer, was also rather discouraged. He had only a handful of bone fragments to show for hours of effort. However, when Dr. Colbert looked closely at these fossil scraps, his excitement was that of a treasure hunter at the first glimpse of his prize. He recognized one piece as a bit of claw. And its size and shape indicated it had belonged to Coelophysis!

The next day the fossil hunters went immediately to the spot where Mr. Whitaker had found the bone. It was a long, sloping cliff where loose rocks slid out from under foot at every step. But as crumbling rock was brushed away, more and more bones began to appear. And almost all were of the long-sought Coelophysis.

Dr. Colbert hurriedly turned his expedition into a large-scale production. A road was made through juniper groves and across a stream so that supplies could more easily be carried to the excavation site, and more people were brought from New York to give assistance.

Since the fragile bones could best be removed from surrounding rock in a laboratory, the task at hand was to cut the sandstone into blocks and ship them to the museum. Doing so presented a problem because the bones lay in an almost solid mass. It was solved by making curved cuts instead of going in a straight line. In some cases bones were carefully chipped out of the sandstone, after first marking their positions on a diagram so that the connection with neighboring fossils would be known exactly.

Encased in plaster of paris, the blocks were dragged by a bulldozer to a point from which they could be sent

A block of bones is encased in plaster of paris and made ready for shipment from New Mexico to New York. *Courtesy, The American Museum of Natural History.*

eastward, and the happy paleontologists went along with them. At last Coelophysis had emerged from its obscure past, and Dr. Colbert could have prepared for exhibition an accurate picture of a dinosaur almost two hundred million years old.

[91]

But today the thoughts of this dedicated scientist are mostly concentrated on the Antarctic. It was Dr. Colbert who sparked plans for a major fossil hunt on that southernmost continent after he was shown a fossil taken from there. He identified it as a piece of an amphibian's jaw.

By the fall of 1969 Dr. Colbert, as part of a team of geologists and paleontologists, was exploring in the frozen sandstone cliffs of Antarctica, and a second expedition returned for a season that spanned 1970 and 1971.

Then excitement reigned! Working in the most rugged conditions, they found an abundance of fossils, showing again and again that two hundred million years ago "Antarctic animals" were similar to animals of other continents.

Now this beginning has been made, who can tell what stories of the past are waiting to be discovered in the land surrounding the South Pole?

11. The Making of a Skeleton

The skeleton of a dinosaur, exhibited in a museum hall, looks impressive—the "framework" of an animal dead and gone for millions of years. And visitors to the museum are impressed. However, unless they know the story behind the skeleton, they are not likely to appreciate all the work involved in putting the bones together.

The "making" of a skeleton might be said to start when the bones arrive in the museum laboratory. But actually the work begins in the collecting field, because unless they were given proper care as they were dug out of the earth, they would not hold together to reach a museum.

As a first step, after dinosaur bones have been partly excavated, they are coated with shellac which fills and hardens cracks. This holds a bone more firmly together. After the shellac has dried, exposed parts of the bone, or bones, are covered with tissue paper and more shellac. Next the upper part of the fossil is covered with strips of burlap dipped in liquid plaster or, sometimes, flour paste.

After the burlap and plaster wrapping has dried and hardened, a trench is dug around the entire fossil, which is then freed from the rock that held it. Now it can be turned over and the bottom given a similar coating treatment. Sometimes wooden planks are used as splints to give further support.

A skeleton may be removed from the earth bone by bone, or taken out in blocks, with each block containing a number of bones. In any case, an accurate diagram is made, on cross-ruled paper, showing exactly how the bones lay when they were found.

Well secured and protected, the fossils are ready for packing in wooden cases, surrounded by straw. But since a single dinosaur bone may weigh two or three hundred pounds, this step is not simple.

Often such prize discoveries are made far away from civilization; therefore it is a long haul to a railroad shipping point. By the time fossils reach their museum destination, months of work may have already been invested in their recovery.

In the laboratory, once the bones have been removed from their plaster and burlap wrappings, more detailed and exacting efforts begin. Each bone must be completely removed from surrounding rock and cleaned. As rock bits

Brontosaurus bones being prepared for shipment by Dr. Walter Granger. *Courtesy, The American Museum of Natural History.*

are chipped away, the fossil is hardened with cement. Often a bone was broken or crushed before it was discovered, and in such cases pieces must be cemented together. Large bones, needing support, are drilled and steel rods inserted into them. Missing parts are filled in with plaster.

When it is decided to use a certain dinosaur for exhibition, a paleontologist may have problems with "missing parts." For example, if it had been impossible to find the

Brontosaurus skeleton being mounted for exhibition at The American Museum of Natural History. *Courtesy, The American Museum of Natural History.*

hind legs of some interesting species, but the rest of the bones are in good condition, a scientist must use his knowledge of similar animals, living and extinct, and his imagination, to "restore" those lost limbs. Of course, if one hind leg is discovered, it is not a major task to create a second.

Once all the bones of an animal have been thoroughly cleaned and treated, a sand table is prepared, large enough to accommodate the skeleton. First the spine is laid out, making sure all the vertebrae fit correctly with each other.

The Making of a Skeleton

The skeleton of Tyrannosaurus fills museum visitors with awe. It seems the ancient bones are almost ready to come alive. *Courtesy, The American Museum of Natural History.*

Then the relationship of the hip bones to the vertebrae is worked out. How the ribs should relate to the vertebrae and the shoulder blades to the ribs, are among other puzzles that must be solved.

The time involved in preparing a skeleton for exhibition may take weeks, months or years, depending on the size of the animal and the condition of its bones. When the remains of a Brontosaurus were sent to the American Museum from Wyoming in 1898, scientists and technicians spent four years putting the skeleton together. But finally it stood in all its magnificent length of sixty-seven feet, ready to impress the world with the size and shape of the thunder lizard.

The skeleton of Diplodocus, the elongated dinosaur that was recovered for the Carnegie Museum, is made up of nearly three hundred bones.

Little dinosaurs, especially those whose bones have been well preserved, of course require nothing like the work needed for the giants. But to bring the prehistoric story to the public, any fossil skeleton must be handled with care, studied by skilled paleontologists, prepared for exhibition by scientists and technicians, and given an interesting label that explains its history.

12. Model Dinosaurs

A dinosaur skeleton, skillfully exhibited, does much to bring the animal "back to life." However, artists and sculptors go well beyond a framework of bones by picturing prehistoric animals in the flesh—as they must have looked in life, eating, fighting, and hunting.

How can an artist actually portray an animal that was never seen by a human being?

He must, of course, have a thorough knowledge of anatomy. With this, he can compare the muscles of a living animal similar in form to one of prehistoric times, and understand how to build on the ancient creature's skeleton. The areas at which muscles are attached to bones (called "muscle scars") have rough surfaces. Muscle scars are very helpful in deciding the size and type muscles had been. After the positions of head, neck, and limb muscles are worked out, the animal's body form is well established.

Skin is compared with that of similar living animals. Because dinosaurs were reptiles, it must be assumed that they had scaly skin as modern reptiles do. This preserves body moisture. Without waterproof scales, body moisture would soon evaporate, causing death. Reptiles do not have sweat glands in their skin.

Very helpful in picturing dinosaur skin have been the discoveries of a mummified dinosaur and fossilized pieces of skin. However, there is no reason to believe that all dinosaurs had the same type of scales or the same coloring. (All types of lizards do not match in coloring or type of scales.)

An artist portraying prehistoric animals works closely with a paleontologist. Charles R. Knight, whose stunning paintings of dinosaurs are to be seen in the great museums of the United States, always did.

Mr. Knight's usual method of working was first to make a small model of the animal to be painted. Seeing it in three dimensions was stimulating to his imagination. Besides, with a model placed in the sunlight, shadows are cast on the ground, creating a life-like atmosphere. He once commented, "I never think of a fossil animal as being dead. At one time it was a living, breathing mechanism, moving about this earth in an atmosphere of color, light, and shade, precisely as a modern animal does."

Models of dinosaurs have been worked out in different ways. One method is to reproduce them in fiber glass. In this fashion a fabulous exhibit of the popular giants—

This fiber-glass model of Stegosaurus was the first of a group of dinosaurs designed and constructed by the Louis Paul Jonas Studios for the World's Fair of 1964–65. The models have been exhibited in many other places since then. *Courtesy, Louis Paul Jonas Studios, Inc.*

Tyrannosaurus, Stegosaurus, and others—was made for the New York World's Fair of 1964–65. The animals were constructed at the Louis Paul Jonas Studios, located close to the Hudson River, about fifty miles from New York City.

Stegosaurus was the first beast to be re-created. Mr. Jonas, a fine sculptor, made a miniature model of the animal. This was cut into thin sections, and the sections served as guides to make a full-size model.

With this accomplished, the clay Stegosaurus was covered with plaster reinforced with burlap and pieces of pipe. When the plaster had dried, it was stripped—in sections —from the clay model, and the sections were given coats of plasticine. They were then fitted together, with an internal steel frame, and the whole animal was bonded with resin and glass cloth. Painting was the final step.

Barnum Brown who, so many years before, found the ancient bones of Tyrannosaurus and other giants, worked with Mr. Jonas and a staff of eighteen skilled assistants at the studios to develop the group of nine "modern" dinosaurs. Two months were spent on creating Stegosaurus alone. This fiber-glass creature was then left outdoors for a year to test its durability. The test was completely successful.

When the models were completed, they were placed on a huge barge and towed down the Hudson River and around lower Manhattan to the fairgrounds on Long Island. It was an astounding sight: Dinosaurs majestically by-passing tug boats, ferries, and ocean liners in the New York harbor.

Just as fossil hunting today is enjoyed by amateurs as well as by experts, so the making of models and plaster casts, besides being a fine art, has become a popular hobby.

Robert Salkin, after taking boys and girls on field trips, enjoys showing them how to make simple plaster casts. If a good fossil has been found—perhaps a dinosaur foot-

Pedro Serrano is interested in paleontology, and likes to create his own dinosaurs with aluminum foil. *Photo by James Staples.*

print—duplicates of it can be produced quite easily. Mr. Salkin explains:

As a first step, a very thin layer of liquid polymer latex should be rubbed on the footprint and piece of stone surrounding it, using the fingertips. With the top surface and all sides of the fossil covered, it should dry in a warm room for about eight hours. Two or three layers of the latex should be applied and dried in the same way. Then a piece of pre-shrunk cheesecloth should be added, on top of which goes another layer of latex. Cheesecloth and latex are repeated until there are five or six layers of latex and two or three of cheesecloth.

The cheesecloth gives the mold a firm body and prevents its stretching out of shape.

When the final coat has hardened (a few days are needed to reach this step) the cheesecloth-latex combination can be peeled off the fossil. It now is a rubber mold.

Ordinary plaster of paris will make the cast. It should be mixed with water, as directed on the package, then poured into the mold. In about thirty minutes it will harden. The rubber mold is then stripped away—and there is a duplicate of the dinosaur footprint. A bit of hand painting may be used to bring out highlights for a more interesting effect.

Anyone who would enjoy making his own models of dinosaurs may do so in a simple, no-fuss, no-muss, way. Aluminum foil is the material to use. The young sculptor should have a knowledge of the lines and proportions of the dinosaur he wishes to portray, and at first make frequent checks with a good picture of his subject.

The aluminum foil can be compacted, pulled loose, snipped with scissors, and otherwise made to conform to

a desired shape. A dinosaur with a simple outline, such
as Brontosaurus, is obviously a better beginning model than
an armored species such as Stegosaurus.

Altogether there are a number of ways in which dinosaurs may become a hobby: Learning about them from
scientists. Studying them in museums. Searching for their
fossilized footprints or bones. Making dinosaur models.

To "find" a dinosaur is not an impossible dream.

DOROTHY E. SHUTTLESWORTH has been exploring nature since she started working for The American Museum of Natural History in New York at the age of seventeen. After several years there on the staff of *Natural History*, she became the first editor of a similar magazine for young people—*Junior Natural History*—a position which she held for twelve years.

Her more recent years have been devoted to writing books—she has authored more than two dozen—and magazine articles on nature, science, and conservation. Besides being a homemaker and mother of a daughter and a son, she is active in community affairs. She lives in East Orange, New Jersey, with her husband.

Index

Cockroaches, 16
Coelophysis, 1, 88–91
Colbert, Dr. Edwin, 25; and discovery of Coelophysis, 88–92; *ill.*, 25
Colorado, 8–10
Como Bluff, Wyo., 42–47
Connecticut River Valley, 5–7
Cope, Edward, dinosaur discoveries of, 40–46, 88
Crested dinosaurs, 70
Cretaceous period, 19, 87
Crinoids, 29
Crocodiles, 16, 19, 22, 23, 24
Custer, General, 42
Cuvier, Baron George, 2
Cycads (palmlike plants), 15

Delaware Water Gap, 29, 35
Dinosaur National Monument, Utah, 48–56
Dinosaurs (*see also* Fossils, dinosaur; Lizards, dinosaurs as; Reptiles, prehistoric, dinosaurs as; specific aspects, discoveries, kinds): anatomy of, 4, 21–22, 99–100 (*see also* specific aspects, dinosaurs, kinds); ancestors ("family tree") of, 20–26; armored, 24, 62, 71, 84; crested, 70; *Dinosauria* and origin of name, 4, 5; disappearance of, 2, 19, 24–26; duck-billed, 13, 24, 59–61 (*see also* Duck-billed dinosaurs); eggs (egg-laying) and, 73–84; footprints, 5–8, 10 (*see also* Footprints [fossilized tracks]); geological history of the earth and, 11–19, 24–26, 85–92; herbivorous and carnivorous, 15–16, 24, 62; hip (reptilian and bird) arrangement in, 4, 22; horned, 24, 62–64, 71, 80; in Mesozoic Era (Age of Reptiles), 14–19 (*see also* Age of Reptiles; Mesozoic Era); models

of, 99–105; plated, 24; skeletons (Tyrannosaurus and other giants), 57–64; skeletons, preparation and exhibiting of, 93–98, 99–105; skin, 60, 61, 70 (*see also* Skin, fossil dinosaur); tail, 62
Diplodocus, 42, 49, 61, 98
Douglass, Earl, 48–56
Dragonflies, 16
Duck-billed dinosaurs, 13, 24, 44, 46, 59–61, 79, 84 (*see also* specific dinosaurs); *ill.*, 60; Trachodon, 59–61

Earth, the, dinosaurs and history of, 11–19, 24–26, 85–92 (*see also* Eras, geologic; Geology, dinosaurs and; specific aspects, eras, locations, periods); continents and land bridges between, 85–92
Earthquakes, 11
Eggs, dinosaur, 24–25, 73–84; *ill.*, 81
England, 39
Eras, geologic, 12, 13; Mesozoic (Age of Reptiles), 14–19, 21, 88 (*see also* Age of Reptiles; Mesozoic Era); Paleozoic, 12–14
Erie Canal, N.Y., 41
Eubrontes, 7
Europe, 22, 73. *See also* specific countries, discoveries, individuals

Ferns, prehistoric, 14, 15
Fiber-glass dinosaur models, 100–2
Flaming Cliffs, 80, 82–83
Flying reptiles (pterodactyls), 16, 26, 39
Footprints (fossilized tracks), 5–8, 10, 30, 31–34; *ill.*, 6; making plaster casts of, 102–4
Fossils, dinosaur, 1–10, 12 (*see also* Dinosaurs; specific aspects, kinds); collecting, hunting, 7–10, 27–39, 40–47, 48–56, 65–72, 73–

Index